World of Reading

LEVEL 2

MARVEL

THOR™
THE DARK WORLD
HEROES OF ASGARD

By TOMAS PALACIOS

Based on a Screenplay by CHRISTOPHER L. YOST

and CHRISTOPHER MARKUS & STEPHEN McFEELY

Story by DON PAYNE and ROBERT RODAT

Produced by KEVIN FEIGE, p.g.a.

Directed by ALAN TAYLOR

Illustrated by RON LIM, CAM SMITH and LEE DUHIG

ABDO
Spotlight

MARVEL

NEW YORK • LOS ANGELES

WWW.ABDOPUBLISHING.COM

Reinforced library bound edition published in 2015 by Spotlight, a division of ABDO
PO Box 398166, Minneapolis, Minnesota 55439. Spotlight produces high-quality
reinforced library bound editions for schools and libraries. Published by Marvel Press,
an imprint of Disney Book Group.

Printed in the United States of America, North Mankato, Minnesota.
052014
072014

THIS BOOK CONTAINS
RECYCLED MATERIALS

marvelkids.com

© 2013 MARVEL

LIBRARY OF CONGRESS CATALOGING-IN-PUBLICATION DATA

This title was previously cataloged with the following information:

Palacios, Tomas.
Thor: the dark world: heroes of Asgard / by Tomas Palacios ; illustrated by Ron Lim,
Cam Smith, and Lee Duhig.
  p. cm. -- (World of reading. Level 2)
1. Thor (Norse deity)--Juvenile fiction. 2. Film novelizations--Juvenile fiction. I. Lim,
Ron, ill. II. Smith, Cam, ill. III. Duhig, Lee, ill. IV. Title. V. Series.
[E]--dc23

2013936920

978-1-61479-263-5 (Reinforced Library Bound Edition)

Spotlight
A Division of ABDO
www.abdopublishing.com

There are all types of creatures and
monsters that live in the Nine Realms.
Some are big and some are small.
Some are good and some are bad.

Sometimes the bigger monsters pick
on the smaller creatures.
That's when the heroes are called!
Hogun the Grim is a part of the
Warriors Three.
He is strong and tough!
He uses his mace to battle
the monsters!

When Hogun needs help he calls on
Fandral the Dashing!
Fandral is the second member of the
Warriors Three.
Fandral rides a white horse!
He flashes his sharp sword to stop
the villains!

Fandral and Hogun need help!
That's when Volstagg arrives!
Volstagg is the third member of the
Warriors Three.
He barrels down on the enemy!
He uses his big ax and swings away!

Now and then even the Warriors
Three need a friend to lend a hand.
That's when Lady Sif arrives!
She is very quick and agile.
Lady Sif spins her bladed sword to
take out the bad guys!

Occasionally, the villains are even stronger than the Warriors Three and Lady Sif combined!
Sometimes they need someone to help all of them.
Who could that be?

Suddenly a portal opens up in the sky.
It is the Bifrost! It is the bridge Asgard
uses to travel from realm to realm.
The Bifrost is very bright!
The villains all run with fear!
They know the Bifrost means trouble!

Something flies out of the Bifrost!
It hits one monster. Then it hits
another!
Volstagg and Lady Sif see what it is.
It is Mjolnir!
Mjolnir is a mighty hammer. It is so
powerful that almost no one can use
it or even hold it.

The hammer takes out most
of the Marauders.
The Warriors Three and
Lady Sif smile.
When they see Mjolnir they know
they will also see a mighty friend!

A towering warrior steps out of
the Bifrost.
It is the Mighty Thor!
Thor is the strongest warrior to ever
live!
He grips his hammer and faces
the villains.
He will put a stop to them and save
the day!

The Warriors Three and Lady Sif
join Thor in the fight!
They bash and smash the monsters!
Thor uses his hammer.
Lady Sif uses her blade.
Fandral uses his sword!
Hogun uses his mace!
Volstagg uses his ax!

They thought the fight was over.
That's when a huge rock monster
appears in front of them!
The creatures laugh and cheer.
The rock monster is their
secret weapon.
They are sure the huge beast
will defeat Thor!

The rock monster is big and strong.
Thor will not back down!
The rock monster charges!
His club is ready to strike!
Thor also charges! Mjolnir is ready to strike as well!
They clash, and there is a huge explosion!

The smoke and dust clear.
The winner is the Mighty Thor!
Thor stands proud and strong.
He has defeated the rock monster and
helped save the day!

Thor, the Warriors Three, and Lady Sif stand side by side.

They help the people and save their land.

With the rock monster and the creatures beaten, they can rebuild and be happy again!

Thor knows more battles will
be coming his way.
Thor and his warriors will
be ready.
They are the heroes of Asgard!